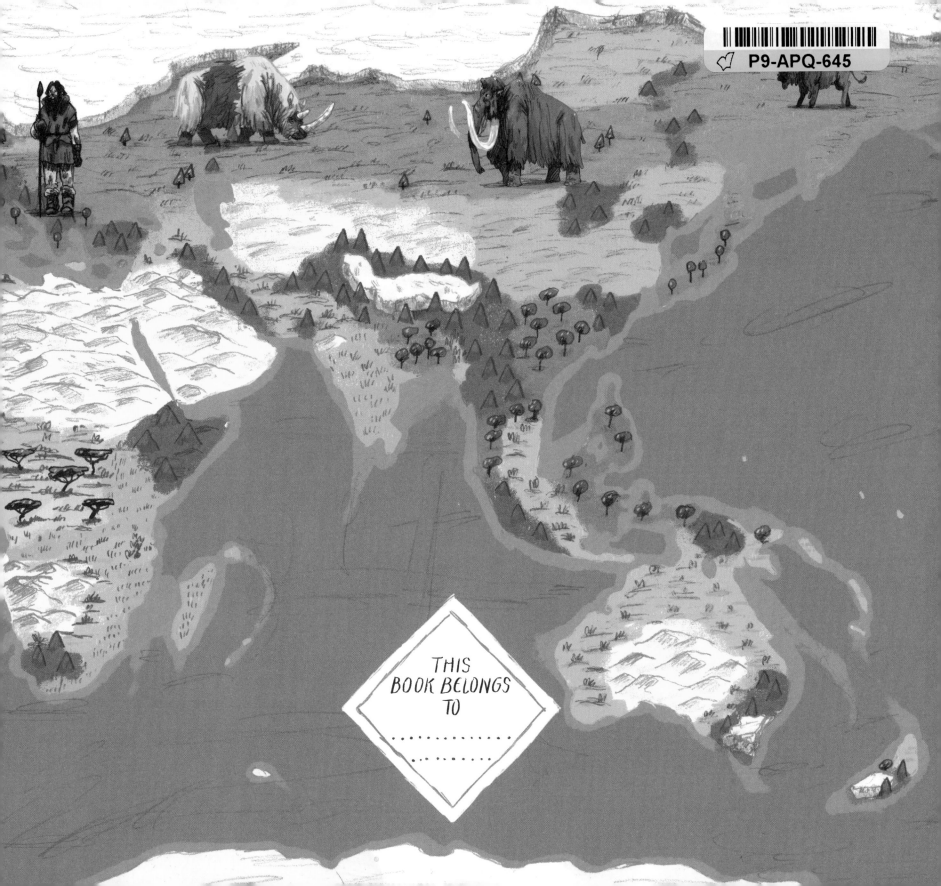

THIS
BOOK BELONGS
TO
. . . .
. . . .

For Helen

Toby and the Ice Giants © Flying Eye Books 2015.

This is a first edition published in 2015 by Flying Eye Books,
an imprint of Nobrow Ltd. 62 Great Eastern Street, London, EC2A 3QR.

Text and illustrations © Joe Lillington 2015.
Joe Lillington has asserted his right under the Copyright,
Designs and Patents Act, 1988, to be identified as the Author of this Work.

Published in the US by Nobrow (US) Inc.
Printed in Belgium on FSC assured paper.

ISBN: 978-1-909263-58-1

Order from www.flyingeyebooks.com

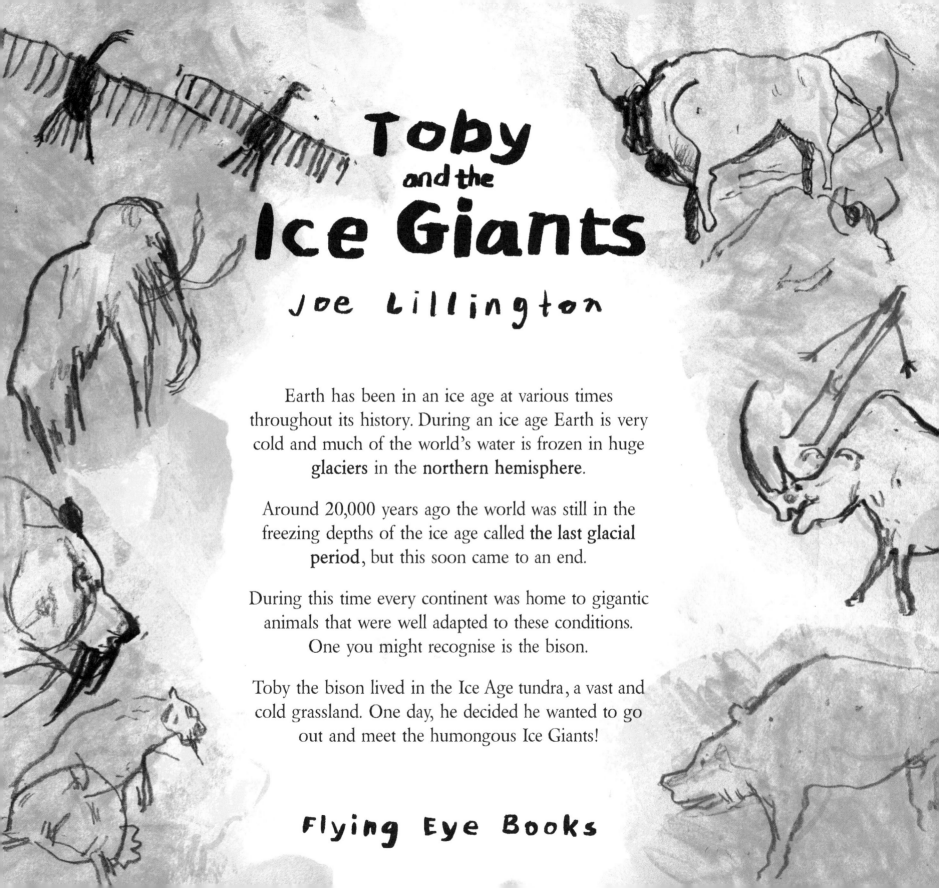

Toby
and the
Ice Giants

Joe Lillington

Earth has been in an ice age at various times throughout its history. During an ice age Earth is very cold and much of the world's water is frozen in huge **glaciers** in the **northern hemisphere**.

Around 20,000 years ago the world was still in the freezing depths of the ice age called **the last glacial period**, but this soon came to an end.

During this time every continent was home to gigantic animals that were well adapted to these conditions. One you might recognise is the bison.

Toby the bison lived in the Ice Age tundra, a vast and cold grassland. One day, he decided he wanted to go out and meet the humongous Ice Giants!

Flying Eye Books

But before he could get very far he bumped into something very hard.

"OUCH!
Watch where
you're going!"

"Sorry!
What are you?
Why is your
horn so big?"

*"I'm a WOOLLY RHINO.
My horn is for fighting with!
Do you want a FIGHT?"*

"No, thanks!"
said Toby.

WOOLLY RHINOCEROS
Coelodonta antiquitatis

Size	3–3.8 m long, 2.2 m tall, 60 cm/90 cm long horn
Weight	2700 kg
Diet	Grasses, sedges and other plants
Habitat	Steppe Tundra and Polar Desert in Northern Europe & Asia
Died out	8,000 years ago

Woolly rhinos were a little larger than white rhinos today and covered in a thick layer of fur to keep warm.

They had much longer horns, which could grow up to one metre long! The woolly rhinos used their horns to fight with each other and to sweep away the winter snow to find food.

"Hello, I'm Toby
Your claws are massive!
Do you want to
fight as well?"

"I'm a megatherium,
Toby. I try not to fight all
that much. I just use my
claws to reach food…"

MEGATHERIUM
Megatherium americanum

Megatherium were a species of ground sloth, related to modern tree sloths. They were much bigger and one of the largest mammals of their time!

They walked on all four legs but could also stand on their back legs, using their tail to balance and reach into the branches of tall trees.

Size	6 m long, 3.4 m standing
Weight	3450 kg
Diet	Leaves, twigs, fruit
Habitat	Arid desert, Savannah, woodlands in South America
Died out	10,000 years ago

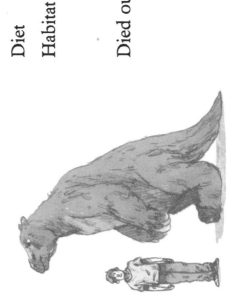

Toby found his way to the sea.

"Being this woolly makes us very itchy. This is how we scratch the itch."

WOOLLY MAMMOTH
Mammuthus primigenius

Size	2.7–3.5 m tall
Weight	3000–5500 kg
Diet	Grasses, sedges and other plants
Habitat	Steppe tundra across North America, Europe and Asia
Died out	4,000 years ago

A woolly mammoth was roughly the same size as an African elephant, but its ears and tail were smaller and they had a thick coat of hair to survive in the cold ice age environment.

Woolly mammoths lived in family groups just like modern elephants, and travelled across most of the **northern hemisphere**.

"Well I'm a Glyptodon and I'm SLOW. You would be too, if you had a heavy shell like mine!"

GLYPTODON

Glyptodon reticulatus

Size	1.5 m tall
Weight	1800 kg
Diet	Grasses and plants
Habitat	North and South America
Died out	11,000 years ago

The Glyptodon was related to modern animals like anteaters and armadillos, but it was much larger.

It evolved a thick shell, like a turtle, to protect itself from **predators**. The shell could be as thick as five centimetres.

SMILODON
Smilodon fatalis

Size	1 m tall, 1.75 m long, 35 cm tail
Weight	160 kg – 280 kg
Diet	Bison, giant ground sloths, possibly young mammoths.
Habitat	North America and coastal South America
Died out	13,000 years ago

Smilodons were top **predators**, evolved to hunt the large animals that lived during the ice age. People often call them sabre-toothed tigers even though they weren't closely related to tigers.

Smilodons were a similar size to modern lions, but were much more muscly. Their teeth were up to eighteen centimetres long, and they could open their mouth twice as wide as a lion can!

"You again, Smilodon? Where are you going?"

"Out of my way you big fat bear, that's MY dinner!"

SHORT-FACED BEAR
Arctodus simus

Short-faced bears were the largest **pleistocene** meat eaters on land, and were larger than any bear alive today.

The short-faced bear's large size meant it had a lot of endurance, which allowed it to travel far and wide to find food from a variety of plants and animals.

Size	1.7 m at shoulder, 3.3 m standing
Weight	1000 kg
Diet	Large animal carcasses, plants, and small animal prey
Habitat	North America
Died out	10,000 years ago

"Phew!"

TERATORN
Aiolornis incredibilis

Size	Wingspan 5 m, 0.75 m standing
Weight	23 kg
Diet	Armadillos, rodent-like mammals, possums, and capybara
Habitat	North America
Died out	10,000 years ago

Aiolornis was the largest flying bird in North America. It had a wingspan of up to 5 metres, making it far larger than the wandering albatross, the bird with the largest wing-span living today.

When hunting Teratorns would use their huge wings to glide over a wide area. Then, once they spotted their target, they would swoop down, grabbing, killing and then eating their prey without even landing!

HUMANS
Homo sapiens

Size	1.8 m
Weight	61 kg
Diet	Meat and some plant foods
Habitat	By this time humans had spread all over the world
Died out	Still around!

Ice age humans looked just like us, but their lifestyle was very different. They hunted and gathered while travelling all over to find food at different times of the year.

Ice age humans were very good hunters and used every part of the animal. Mammoth furs, tusks and bones helped to create their shelters, and they were able to stitch furs together to make clothes to keep warm.

Humans had begun to domesticate dogs, which were very helpful for guarding camps and using their acute sense of smell while hunting.

"Back already Toby?
How was your big adventure?"

"Maybe I'll just stay with
you for now...

BISON
Bison antiquus

Size	2.1–2.3 m tall, 4.6 m long, horn width 1 m tip to tip
Weight	450 kg
Diet	Grasses sedges and other plants
Habitat	North America
Died out	8,000 years ago

Sometimes called the ancient bison, they were the direct **ancestor** of the living American bison today.

Bison live in herds and during the ice age they lived among woolly mammoths, woolly rhinos and other **megafauna**.

After surviving until modern times, bison were almost wiped out in the 19th century because of overhunting, where huge herds of bison were killed at a time. However, thanks to conservation efforts bison are now recovering to large numbers again.

...At least until I'm a bit bigger."

Around 10,000 years ago, **the last glacial period** came to an end. Many of the amazing animals that had lived during this time died out.

Palaeontologists believe the cause of their extinction was partly due to the change in climate and plants. Overhunting by early humans then pushed the struggling populations to extinction.

5 M

4 M

How big are you compared to
the giants of the Ice Age?

3 M

2 M

1 M

| YOU! | TOBY
1 m | TERATORN
0.75 m
5 m Wingspan | SMILODON
1 m | GLYPTODON
1.5 m | SHORT-FACED
BEAR
1.7 m
3.3 m standing |

RLY MAN
1.8 m

WOOLLY
RHINOCEROS
2.2 m

EARLY BISON
2.3 m

MEGATHERIUM
3.4 m

WOOLLY
MAMMOTH
3.5 m

These are some of the other amazing ice age
animals that Toby didn't get to meet!

IRISH ELK
Megaloceros giganteus

GIANT TAPIR
Megatapirus augustus

MASTODON
Mammut americanum

GIANT BEAVER
Castoroides leiseyorum

MACRAUCHENIA
Macrauchenia patachonica

PROTEMNODON
Protemnodon anak

CAVE HYENA
Crocute crocuta spelaea

GENYORNIS
Genyornis newtoni

MEGALANIA
Megalania prisca